GOODNIGHT FORTNITE

A parody to make them to stop playing and go to bed

By Sean Percival

With illustrations by
Sofie Engstrom

Web: www.goodnightfortnite.com

Email: book@goodnightfortnite.com

Author: Sean Percival

Illustrations: Sofie Engstrom

This book is dedicated to Quinn for all those nights of "Just one more match, please Dad!".

DROP

In the great blue room

there was a chest and

a supply drop balloon

Sofie Engstrom

And a painting of

the visitor rocketing

over the moon

And there was

three cuddle bears

And two

sweaty try hards

And a pair

of total bots

And a little

dog house

And a slurp pot

and a durburger

And a bush

And a squad leader

whispering “hush”

Goodnight cube

Sofie Engstrom

Goodnight visitor

rocketing over

the moon

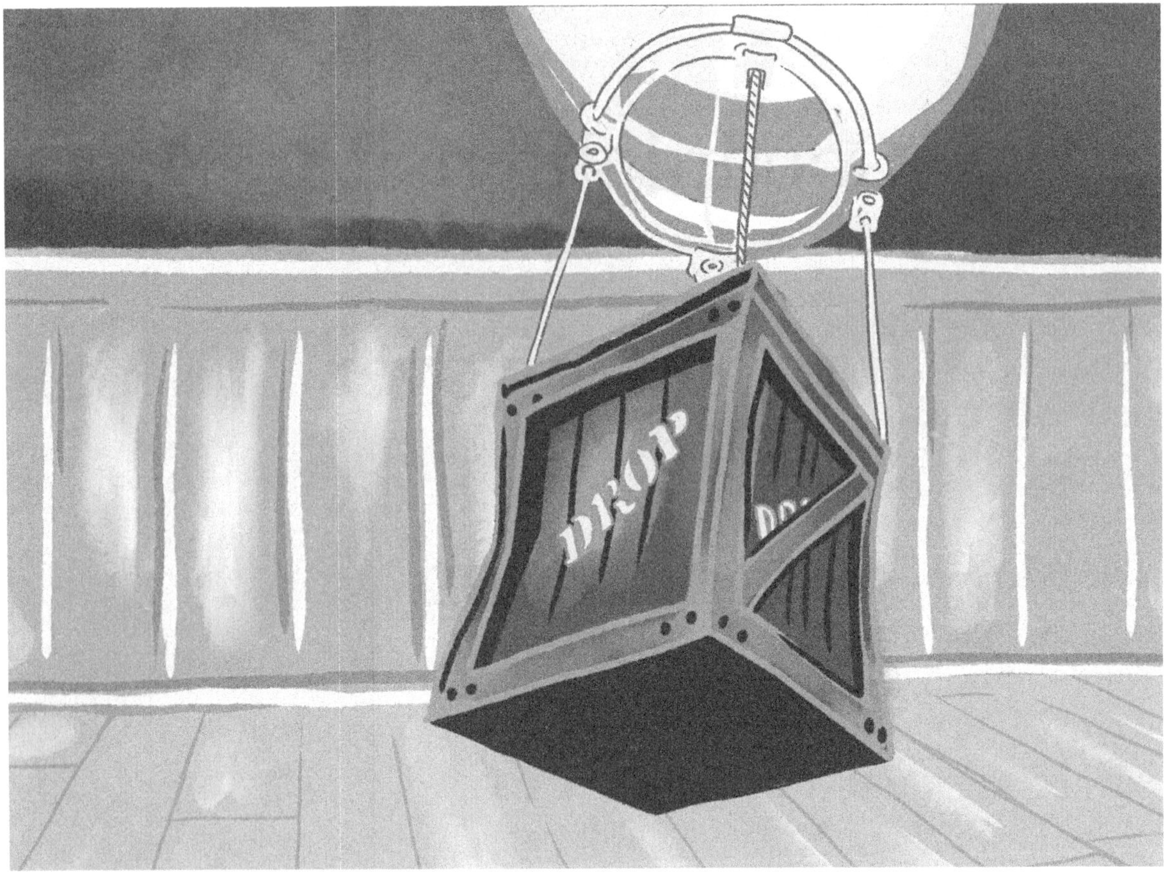
DROP

And the

supply drop

balloon

Goodnight

cuddle bears

Goodnight

chairs

Goodnight

try hards

building stairs

Goodnight

bots

goodnight

bush

And goodnight

squad leader

whispering “hush”

Goodnight

battle stars

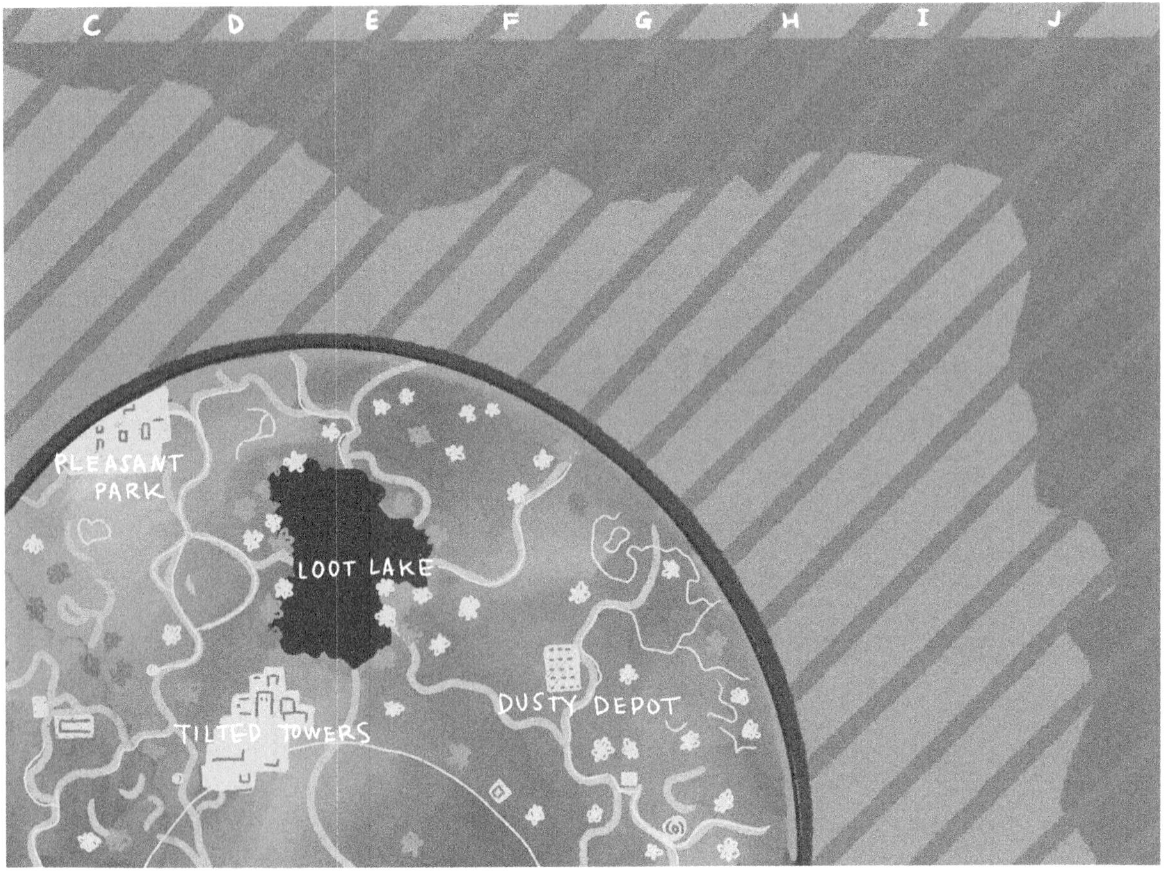
C
D
E
F
G
H
I
J
PLEASANT PARK
LOOT LAKE
TILTED TOWERS
DUSTY DEPOT

Goodnight storm

Good night

footstep noises

everywhere...

...now go to bed!

Made in the USA
Coppell, TX
21 December 2020

46323869R00031